Andrew's Boring Life

by Carey Peters
illustrated by Ilene Richard

Harcourt
SCHOOL PUBLISHERS

Printed in China

ISBN 10: 0-15-350489-7
ISBN 13: 978-0-15-350489-1

Ordering Options
ISBN 10: 0-15-350333-5 (Grade 3 Below-Level Collection)
ISBN 13: 978-0-15-350333-7 (Grade 3 Below-Level Collection)
ISBN 10: 0-15-357475-5 (package of 5)
ISBN 13: 978-0-15-357475-7 (package of 5)

3 4 5 6 7 8 9 10   985   12 11 10 09 08

Andrew threw himself onto the couch and sighed. "How was school today?" Dad asked.

"All right, I guess," Andrew replied. "We're doing a project with a school in the United States. We have to write letters to pen pals. It's so bothersome."

"That sounds like fun," said Dad.

"I don't have anything to write about," said Andrew.

"Tell about your life here," Dad said.

"There's nothing special about my life," sighed Andrew.

"Your pen pal might not think so," said Dad. "Do you want to hear about life in the United States?"

4

"Yes," said Andrew.

"Then your pen pal probably feels the same way," said Dad. "Now let's go pick up Mom. She dropped her car at the garage for repairs. The din coming from the engine was loud."

Andrew sat down that night and began to write.

December 5

Dear Sophie,

I'm Andrew, your new pen pal. I live in Sydney, Australia. I have an older brother named Max, a dog, and a cat.

It's almost summer here. I go to the beach every day now. Max is teaching me to surf. He wins surfing contests!

I also like to play rugby and cook. My favorite class in school is science.

Your pen pal,
Andrew

Mr. Flynn mailed the letters, and everyone's pen pal wrote back quickly.

December 17

Dear Andrew,

Thanks for writing. I live in Franklin, Tennessee. I have a brother, too, but he is only four. We have two cats. I like horses, and I like to ride.

It's summer there now? It's winter here!
I've seen kangaroos and koalas at the zoo.
Have you ever seen them outside a zoo?

What is Sydney like? Your life sounds very
exciting. Please write back soon!

Your pen pal,
Sophie

Dear Sophie,

Sydney is a large city. People from all over the world come here. My mom speaks Japanese and French. Sometimes she translates for tourists.

I've never seen kangaroos in the city. They are everywhere else, though. You might see them dodging cars along the road.

Once I tried to catch a kangaroo. I ran very hard. My chest was heaving and my legs hurt, but it still easily hopped away.

Your pen pal,
Andrew

Andrew wrote letters every week. He and
Sophie talked about school. They talked
about family. Andrew told her about places
he and his family had visited.

"How's your pen pal?" Dad asked one day.

"She's fine," replied Andrew.

"You must have found something to write," Dad said.

"Sophie has lots of questions. She even says my life is exciting," said Andrew.

Dad laughed, "I guess it must be then."

February 1

Dear Sophie,

Thank you for the picture. Wow, that horse is big!

We visited a koala rescue station. Here is a picture of me with a baby koala.

Mr. Flynn says the class project is over, but I hope we can keep writing. I used to think my life was boring. Now you've made me see that it isn't!

Your friend,

Andrew

Think Critically

1. When does Andrew tell about his visit to the koala rescue station?

2. Why is Andrew writing letters to Sophie?

3. Why does Sophie think Andrew's life is more interesting than he does?

4. Do you think kangaroos are fast? Why or why not?

5. Do you think Andrew's life seems interesting? Why or why not?

 Social Studies

All About Australia You learned a bit about Australia from Andrew's letters. First, find Australia on a globe. Then, make a list of what you learned about Australia from the story on a sheet of paper.

 School-Home Connection Tell a family member what you learned about Australia from this story.

Word Count: 517